SIX MAGICAL FOLK TALES

Retold and illustrated by
Robert Sargent

To Tore, Kate, and Richard

Lancelot
press

Contents

The King's New Room
A TALE FROM RUSSIA

A king who lived in the greatest castle in northern Russia had so much money and so many jewels and gold ornaments that the rooms of his castle were filled to the ceilings, and he hardly had a place to sit down.

One day he decided to have a new room built onto the back of the castle — a room in which he would put his most precious things.

And so an announcement was made that the king was searching for a man who could build a very large room.

Now in the village below the castle, there happened to be a carpenter who had always envied the king's riches. When he heard of the new room which was to be built, this carpenter went to the king and offered his services.

"Have you ever built anything this large before?" the king asked the man.

"Oh yes, sire," answered the man. "On an island in one of the southern lakes, I built a large tower."

"Splendid," exclaimed the king. "Then you have experience." And so the man was given this important job.

He was a very skilled carpenter and he worked night and day to make the large room for the king. But, unknown to the king, the greedy man carefully made a secret passageway in a corner of the new room. On the outside wall of the room he covered the passageway with a large stone that could be rolled away.

The new room had only one door, and that door led directly to the king's chambers. To the king, the new room seemed to be the safest place in the whole castle, for surely no one would dare to go through the king's own bedroom to steal the king's own treasures!

When the room was finished, the king thanked the man and gave him a small chest of gold for his good work. Then the king filled the new room with all his possessions.

Several months went by. Every day the carpenter in the village below the castle thought more and more about the great stone which could be rolled away.

One night he climbed the hill to the castle and very quietly rolled the stone aside and entered the great room. He took the first things that he found, and then he quickly crawled out through the hole in the wall and rolled the stone back in place.

Each night thereafter, the greedy man climbed the hill and stole more of the king's treasures.

At first the king did not notice that anything was missing, for the room was still so full. But then one day he went into the room to look for his Sunday crown and discovered that it was gone. The king became enraged.

He ordered three guards to stand duty in the treasure room every day and every night.

The man in the village did not return to the castle when he heard of the guards posted in the treasure room. But after some time, he began to feel his old hunger for the king's riches. And so one night, when it was very, very late, he climbed the hill again.

The guards were fast asleep when he rolled the stone aside and peered in.

Carefully, he climbed over their feet and took a large jeweled crown. The guards did not even awaken when he rolled the stone back into place.

The next day the king discovered that the crown had been stolen, and he ordered the guards to be imprisoned.

Then he called the court sorcerer to his chambers.

"Someone or something is taking my dearest possessions from the new room," he complained. "You must look into your crystal ball and tell me if you see a bat, a goblin, or a witch who is the thief, because no one human can pass through a locked door without the guards seeing him."

The sorcerer took out his crystal ball and scowled and dusted it off, and said a few special words which made it glow a little.

After a few minutes, the sorcerer said, "I'm afraid it is a human, your highness. The crystal ball shows a man not unlike the very one who built the room."

"But how does he enter?" cried the king, in astonishment.

"Through a small opening in the outside wall," said the sorcerer.

The king frowned and scratched his beard in deep thought.

"Well, then, if it is a trick he is playing on me, it is a trick he shall receive in return, for I cannot let this go on. Can you help me?"

The sorcerer sent for a pair of boots. Then, from a pouch which he kept hidden inside his cap, he sprinkled several grains of magic dust over the boots.

"Give these to the fellow as a gift," said the sorcerer, "and your troubles will be ended."

The next day the king called the carpenter to the castle.

"I am so happy with the beautiful new room you built for me that I wish to reward you with these wonderful boots which I have had made especially for you," the king said.

When he arrived home, the man put the new boots on. But no sooner had he paraded about the house, gloating over his luck, than his feet began to itch! First they itched just a little down near the toes. Then they itched across the soles of his feet—and then they itched up around the ankles, all the way to the tops of the boots! Desperately, he tried to pull the boots off. But they were too tight.

The itching became worse and worse. Then the boots wouldn't let the man sit still or stand still!

The man was very, very tired, and he leaned on one of the king's gold chests to rest. And at that moment, the itching stopped!

The man was very surprised. When he took his hand away from the chest, the itching began again! That night the man was able to sleep only because he held one of the king's crowns in his hands all through the night.

The next morning the man tried to cut the boots off. No matter how he tried, he couldn't pull them off or cut them off. And whenever he stepped away from the king's treasures, the itching began again.

"The king has given me boots with a magic spell!" he realized. "If I am to stop the itching, I must hold one of his possessions. But if I am holding one of the king's possessions, I cannot enter the streets of the village. I can't even leave this room! Perhaps if I return the treasures to the new room, the king will forgive me and free me from this torture!"

Late that very night, the carpenter loaded his wagon and returned to the castle. He could hardly keep quiet because his feet itched and danced. Only when the last gem and crown had been put back into place, did the itching stop. Quietly the man pushed the great rock back against the wall. Then, much relieved, he returned home.

This time, when he attempted to pull the boots off, he had no trouble at all. But just in case the boots might start their magic again, the man wore sandals from that time on—and never again was he attracted to the property of others.

The Beautiful Bird
A TALE FROM MEXICO

One day a poor young farmer came by the gardens of a rich land-owner and, upon passing the gate, he looked in at the lovely flowers there.

Just as he turned to go away, he saw the daughter of the land-owner sitting by herself, singing songs of love. The daughter was so beautiful, that he felt happiness and sorrow at the same time.

His happiness was for the beauty of the daughter, and his sorrow was that he knew he was too poor to ever win her hand in marriage. Certainly the father of the girl would not allow her to even speak to a poor farmer boy.

Then he got an idea.

The very next day he went to a lady who was known throughout the countryside for her magical powers.

The lady listened to the farmer boy's story and she agreed that he was in no position to ask for the hand of the landowner's daughter. But she felt the boy should at least talk to the girl and learn the girl's own wishes. So the lady cooked a special broth and told the young man to drink it.

"You will turn into a beautiful bird and you can then fly into the garden and sing to her," she said. "If the girl becomes interested in someone else, or something else, then you will remain a bird that can only sing. If the girl is interested in your song and has eyes for no other, you will be able to talk to her and learn if she likes you."

Now the father of the daughter wanted her to meet someone of high position and great wealth, and so he had been inviting several wealthy gentlemen to visit her. While everyone fell in love with her, none of them really caught her interest.

"My daughter must make the final choice herself. I will not have her unhappy," he would tell the callers.

One day a very, very rich man came to visit, and he talked of many wonderful things that he planned to do in the future. At first the daughter listened to him with great interest because it seemed that he was sincere. But then when he came again and again and repeated his wonderful plans over and over, it was obvious that he was just making idle talk. The daughter became very bored with her suitor.

Then one day a beautiful bird flew into the garden and the daughter was so happy with this new visitor that she watched it and listened to its song and paid less and less attention to her suitor.

After several days of being thus ignored, the very, very rich man became jealous. The next day he hid in the garden, and with his long rifle he shot at the bird.

The daughter ran crying to her father, and the rich man was told to leave their home and never to return again.

The bird had sung very beautifully, but when the rifle shot passed so close to it, it became frightened and lost its voice.

The daughter was sad, for she understood why the bird could not sing. Each day she waited eagerly for its arrival. The silent little bird would flit and hop and sit on the garden bath, and the girl would sing to it.

The father had invited other young men to meet his daughter, but the girl told her father, of all the visitors to the garden, she loved the bird most.

"Perhaps the bird isn't good for you," he said. "It has made you uninterested in everything else."

"It is beautiful, and I love it," said the girl. "If it could speak to me I would be so happy. It comes every day to my garden, even after someone has shot at it. It is very devoted."

When the bird heard this, he flew back to the lady who had cast the magic spell. He wanted her to know that the landowner's daughter loved him, and that he loved her.

But he could not speak.

At first the lady did not see him because he could not call out, so he fluttered against her window and finally attracted her attention. Realizing that something had happened to the bird, she cooked another broth and made him drink it.

This second magic broth brought back the young man's voice, and he told her how the daughter looked every day for him and was not interested in other visitors.

"Fine!" said the lady. "The next time you enter the garden, you must hide among the flowers. You will be able to talk to her, but she must not see you there. Ask her if her feelings would be the same if you were not a beautiful bird, but a farmer boy instead."

So the beautiful bird flew into the garden and hid in the flowers just behind the chair where the daughter usually sat.

Soon the girl came into the garden and waited for the bird.

Then a voice spoke clearly from behind her.

"Do not look for me, please," spoke the bird. "I must know how you feel about me. As a beautiful bird you have looked for me every day. Would you do so if I were an ugly toad?"

The girl laughed. "What a silly question! Friendship is deeper than that!"

"What if I was a poor farmer who lived down the road?" asked the bird.

"I would love you even more," laughed the girl, "but I'm not unhappy that you are a bird."

At that moment the beautiful bird was so happy that he shook all over, and suddenly his feathers fell out and he turned back into the farmer boy.

The daughter brought him to her father, and together they told him the story.

Her father was so glad to see his daughter happily in love with someone who was not a bird, that he agreed to their marriage. And so they were married, and they moved to a newly built farmhouse and, as you may have guessed, they were happy ever after.

The Giant's Garden
A TALE FROM GREECE

Once, a long time ago, a giant lived in a large villa with a garden surrounded by high walls. While it was very beautiful, the giant's house stood in the worst possible place, for it directly blocked a main road. Poor travelers, with their carts and their bundles and their baskets of food, found it very difficult to get through the narrow pass near the giant's house.

One day, when the sun was very warm and the land had become so dry that every footstep caused clouds of dust, a beggar stopped at the gate of the giant's house and rang the bell.

"Your garden looks so cool and the fruit within so refreshing, that I could not help but ask if you would allow me to rest a moment in the shade," he said.

The giant had heard stories of how some people stole fruit from gardens when the owners weren't looking. So he answered, "My garden is not a public park. You cannot come in."

The beggar went wearily along to the end of the road, and there he came to the house of the gods. He knocked at their door and was admitted immediately.

"What seems to be the trouble?" asked the gods, kindly.

"Should not those who <u>have</u> share with those who do not have?" asked the beggar.

"Yes," replied the gods. "Good fortune is a gift extended only to those worthy of it."

Then the beggar told the sad story of the giant and his garden.

The gods were disturbed. Nothing written in the rules of life proclaimed selfishness as a virtue. After thinking how to deal with the situation, the gods decided to send one of their young messengers to the giant's house, disguised as a beggar.

The messenger appeared at the gate of the giant's garden. He asked the giant for kindness, for the road was hot and he needed to rest in the shade.

The giant became very angry.

"You are the second one who has come to beg my possessions! Go away before I step on you!" he shouted.

Then the gods' messenger said, "Those who are not willing to share what they have, do not deserve to have anything!" He raised his hands, and a green mist rose from the ground. The walls of the garden crumbled into dust, and the giant turned to stone. His beard and his hair spread into shady, cool forests, and his house became a high cliff with tumbling waterfalls.

From that time on, this beautiful resting place has given weary travelers comfort and refreshment on their journeys, and all who pause there are thankful for the shade of the trees and the cool water of the streams.

The Handcarved Mirror
A TALE FROM NORWAY

One summer day, a man who lived in the north of Norway decided to make the long journey over the mountains and along the high coastal road, to the city of Oslo, in the south.

He packed a few of his belongings into a sack, and tied the sack to his shoulders, and started off.

Now the man's father was a wood-carver, and his grandfather had been a wood-carver, and he himself had been a wood-carver since he was a child. So, as he walked along the road, he naturally whittled away at his carvings.

First he carved a bear, and then he carved a rabbit. When he was halfway to Oslo, he found some beautiful birch trees and, selecting one of the best branches, he decided to carve a frame for a hand mirror.

He worked on it day and night and he made one of the most beautiful frames ever seen, with animals and flowers and stars and trees all carefully carved on the handle.

One night, when the man had fallen asleep by the roadside, a tiny little elf came out of a tree nearby and looked at the lovely carvings. The bear seemed so lifelike that at first the elf was afraid! Then he saw the rabbit and the other animals the man had carved, and he became very excited and ran to get another elf to come and look.

"Aren't they wonderful!" exclaimed the first elf.

"Very fine, indeed!" agreed the second elf.

Then, reaching boldly into the man's sack, they pulled out the almost finished carving of the mirror frame.

"Ooooooooh!" they gasped together.

"That is the most beautiful handle I have ever seen," said the second elf.

"When the mirror is put into it, it will be marvelous!" said the first elf.

Then with a snap of his fingers, the first little elf pulled a mirror glass out of his pocket. When he placed it next to the frame, he saw that it would fit perfectly!

"I didn't know you had a mirror glass!" cried the second elf.

"Well," replied the first, "it was my grandmother's and it's so old that it has almost lost its spell. It is really only good for just one more wish, so I might as well give it to the wood-carver who made such beautiful things."

Gently they rested the glass near the sack so that the man would find it first thing in the morning. Then quietly they returned to their homes in the trees.

In the morning, when the man had rubbed his eyes and brushed his hair, he looked down at his carvings and wondered how they had fallen out of his sack. While he was putting them away, he found the mirror glass.

"That will make a fine mirror for my frame," he said, smiling. Much to his surprise, it fitted perfectly.

That day the man walked the last part of the journey and arrived in the city of Oslo, where he learned that a great ball was to be held that very night in the king's castle, and that everyone was invited.

The wood-carver sat quietly in the park, thinking about his long journey and about how much it would mean to him to meet the king.

When he went to the bakery to buy bread for his lunch, he told the lady there how happy he was that he had arrived in time for the ball.

"But you can't wear those clothes to the ball!" she cried.

"They are the only clothes I have," said the man.

"You must buy others!" exclaimed the lady. "After all, to meet the king, we must all dress up!"

The man said that he had only his carvings to sell, and he didn't believe that they would bring him enough money to buy the new clothes needed for the king's ball.

"Well," said the lady, "then you can't go. They would never let you in."

The man returned to his sitting place in the park and tried to think of ways to get new clothes. After he had eaten his bread and cakes, he took out his handsome mirror and started to carve the last little animal for the frame. It was a butterfly which looked as though it had just flown through the air and stopped, for a moment, to rest on the mirror.

As the wood-carver looked into the mirror at himself, he said, "I wish there was some way that I could find the money to buy new clothes. Then I would really be welcome at the king's ball."

Just then a very dignified man and his wife came along and, seeing the carved animals on the ground, they stopped to examine the wood-carver's work.

"That is a beautiful mirror frame you are carving," the wife said to the man. "Is it for sale?"

"If I could get the right price for it," replied the wood-carver.

"And what is the right price for such fine work?" asked the woman's husband.

"I need to buy a suit of clothes so that I may go to the king's ball tonight," said the wood-carver.

"Well," smiled the wife, "my husband and I are tailors, and if you will come to our shop we will be happy to exchange a fine new suit for such a beautiful mirror."

So it was that the magic mirror gave its last wish to the wood-carver. Just as the elf had predicted.

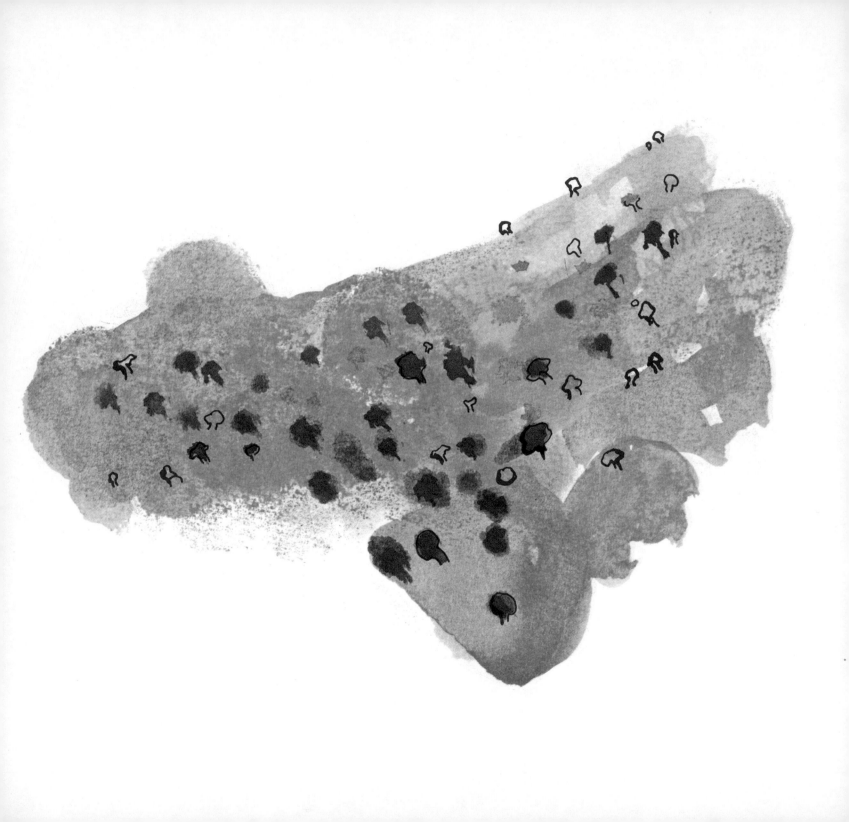

The Magic Bottle
A TALE FROM IRELAND

A farmer who lived in a green valley in Ireland was told one day, by his only daughter, of her desire to marry a young man from the nearby village.

When the farmer saw how happy his daughter was, he gave his consent, but he became very concerned, for he did not have much money and he knew it would be expensive to buy the proper wedding clothes for his only child.

Now hundreds of mushrooms grew in their green valley, and if one took the time to basket them, they brought a good price in the market. The farmer called his daughter, and together they worked for two days, from dawn 'till dark, picking the best mushrooms they could find. Then they loaded the small baskets into their wagon. Early the next morning the farmer hitched his horse to the wagon and started off for the market in the village.

As he turned a bend in the road, where the great pine trees stretch their branches low over the knoll, he saw a curious-looking fellow lying in the middle of the way.

The farmer stopped to find out if he was sleeping there, or if perhaps he was ill, but the fellow didn't move an eyelash, and that worried the farmer.

The little man was pale, and the farmer thought he had fainted, so he got down and lifted the fellow gently onto the back of the wagon, right along with the mushrooms. The farmer thought he would take the little man to the doctor in the village where the market was.

The farmer had not driven long, when he felt a tapping on his shoulder. The little fellow had awakened.

"Where am I?" he asked.

"You're on my wagon, going to town," the farmer replied. "You didn't look well, so I'm taking you to the doctor."

"Oh, I don't need a doctor!" exclaimed the fellow. "I was just a little faint because I hadn't eaten. You see, I only like mushrooms, but someone had picked all the best ones before I could get to them."

"Well," said the farmer, "my daughter and I picked them and, as a matter of fact, I am bringing them to the market now."

"Then you certainly won't mind if I just nibble on a few," answered the fellow, "just to get my strength back."

"I'm truly sorry," replied the farmer, "but I must sell them all to get enough money to buy my daughter her wedding dress. I wish I could spare some for you, but I really cannot."

The little fellow took out a small red bottle and drank from it. "I'll give you my lovely red bottle for one of the baskets," he offered.

But the farmer thanked him kindly and refused the bargain.

As the wagon rolled on, the little fellow became silent and the farmer did not look back, hoping he was asleep and would not ask for mushrooms again.

But the little fellow was not asleep. He nibbled a few mushrooms and, upon tasting how delicious they were, he just couldn't stop! He began to throw whole baskets of mushrooms to the roadside, for eating later on. He did it so quietly that the farmer never heard a sound.

When the last basket had been thrown into the bushes, the little fellow hopped off, himself.

When the farmer arrived at the marketplace, he stopped the wagon to unload. But much to his surprise, the mushrooms were all gone, and the curious little fellow was gone, too!

The only thing in the wagon was a tiny red bottle.

Sadly, the farmer returned home.

That evening, the farmer told his daughter how he had been tricked, and showed her the bottle the little fellow had left behind.

The daughter began to cry. Then she asked her father what the little man looked like, so that she might recognize him if he came into the marketplace in the future.

"Oh, he was sort of greenish and sickly looking, and he wore a tall cap with a bell on it," said the farmer, "and if I ever find him again, it will be the last trick he will ever play on me!"

The daughter asked, "Where, exactly, on the road did you see him?"

"By the pines," came the answer.

The daughter then realized that the fellow must have been one of the magical people who are known to live in the pines.

"Why, father, he must be one of the Pine People," she said excitedly, "and they are usually honest, even when playing tricks!"

Then she took the little man's red bottle, uncorked it, and looked inside. Two drops remained in the bottom. Turning it upside down, she let the drops drain out onto the ground.

Suddenly a puff of smoke appeared in the very spot! When it had blown away, a small chest rested in its place!

Quickly the farmer opened it.

Inside the chest lay a beautiful wedding dress and silver slippers!

The daughter was so excited that she dropped the little red bottle. It broke into many small pieces at her feet.

"It is the most beautiful dress in the world!" she cried, and ran inside to try it on.

Little by little, the tiny pieces of the bottle sank into the ground, unnoticed.

A few days before the wedding, the farmer found a rosebush growing on that same spot! Hundreds of beautiful blossoms flowered on the little bush, and they became the bridal bouquet.

From that time on, the farmer left the mushrooms for the magical people who live in the pines, and no one ever again fainted in front of his cart.

Wahoo's Dream
AN AMERICAN INDIAN TALE

Wahoo felt the time had come for him to travel out into the great forest alone to prove to his father that he could be a great hunter, like the other Indian braves who had gone before him.

Wahoo was small for the age of seven winters, and his father had told him to wait until the next birth of blue flowers appeared under the pines before he made this journey.

But each day Wahoo's desire for his first hunt became stronger and stronger.

"What will you hunt, my son?" asked his father.

"Bear or bison," said Wahoo confidently. "Nothing but the biggest, the wildest, and the most difficult animals!"

"And where will you find these great animals?" asked his father.

"In the great forest where the moon comes from," answered Wahoo.

His father sat silently before the wigwam, and Wahoo waited impatiently for permission to go.

Gradually his father's eyes narrowed as they studied him.

"Would you not think to try something smaller on this hunt?" he asked.

Wahoo stared at him, disbelieving what he had just heard.

"Smaller!" whispered Wahoo. "Smaller is too easy!"

After a few minutes of silence, Wahoo's father spoke again.

"I have not seen such large animals as you speak of in this forest. Would it not be better to concentrate only on what is nearby?"

"You will see, father. I will bring back only the biggest."

"Then, my son, you must not wait any longer." His father smiled. "May the Good Spirit protect you."

That same night, with the arrows his father gave him and a bow he had fashioned, himself, from a young ash tree, Wahoo started off. The moon shone brightly across the fields as he walked as silently as possible into the forest. The great forest enveloped him. At times nothing moved. Then a squirrel would leap in the branches above his head, or a rabbit would dart across his path. But not once did a bear or bison disturb the quiet around him.

Wahoo walked and walked and walked. The next day, when the openings of the leaves above shone bright yellow, Wahoo reached a pool of silver fish, where he bent to take a cool drink.

Just then two rabbits appeared on the knoll directly across the pool from him.

Wahoo thought that he might practice his hunting skills on them. Carefully he pulled his arrow into place. Steadying his arm, he took aim. For a moment, the rabbits stood silently watching. Then each hopped off the rock in opposite directions. Wahoo's arrow sailed over the pool of silver fish and landed on the rock.

"The Good Spirit must not be with me," thought Wahoo.

Just then a fish leaped high out of the pool. Quickly Wahoo jumped forward. He splashed into the pool over the slippery rocks and cornered a small silver fish in shallow water. With great difficulty, he finally caught it.

As he lifted the fish out of the water, Wahoo heard it cry out! He could not believe his ears!

"Please let me go," cried the fish. "I'm far too small and will not make a worthwhile dinner."

"I do not want you for my dinner," said Wahoo. "I want to bring you back to my father so he will not be ashamed of my first day at hunting—even though you are not a bear, or a bison, or even a rabbit."

"But," pleaded the fish, "if you are searching for bigger game I can help you."

"Do not pretend that you can catch what I cannot!" cried Wahoo.

"I said I could help you—if you do not eat me and do as I tell you."

Wahoo thought for a moment and finally agreed.

"Lay me down on that rock over there next to the shore," directed the fish. Gently Wahoo did so.

"Now," said the fish, "you must hide in the bushes nearby."

So Wahoo picked up his bow and arrows and, pulling the leaves apart, climbed into the bushes.

"Do not move," the fish called out. "And when you see a big animal arrive, be sure to shoot when I flip my tail."

So Wahoo hid silently in the bushes and waited and waited and waited.

The sun came down through the openings in the trees above and shone on the rocks in the pool. The silver fish reflected brightly on the rock. Wahoo could smell its delicious odor. Then, quite suddenly, he heard something pushing through the bushes nearby.

Turning his head, Wahoo saw a great bear coming toward the pool. Obviously the bear had smelled the fish lying on the rock in the sun.

As the bear stepped up to the rock, Wahoo raised his arrow to his bow and, pulling the string back as far as possible, took careful aim.

The bear sniffed the air carefully. Seeing the little fish, it moved in closer.

Then the little fish flipped its tail!

ZING!! Wahoo's arrow sailed into the bear! The little fish flipped once more and slid off the rock into the water.

The big bear was dead!

Wahoo was so excited that he hopped out of the bushes and, forgetting his arrow and his bow, and forgetting even to thank the little silver fish, he turned and ran as fast as he could to the path leading back to camp.

When he arrived at the wigwam, he could hardly catch his breath.

"The big bear is dead!" he cried.

His father did not speak at first.

"Where is this big bear?" he finally asked.

"I could not carry it," Wahoo said. "It is just as I dreamed it would be."

So with some disbelief and much talk and wonder, Wahoo's father and six other braves returned to the forest with Wahoo. Finally, they came to the pool with the silver fish. There on the shore lay the large dead bear.

From that day on, Wahoo went out with the hunting parties, and there has always been much talk over the size of Wahoo's first bear.